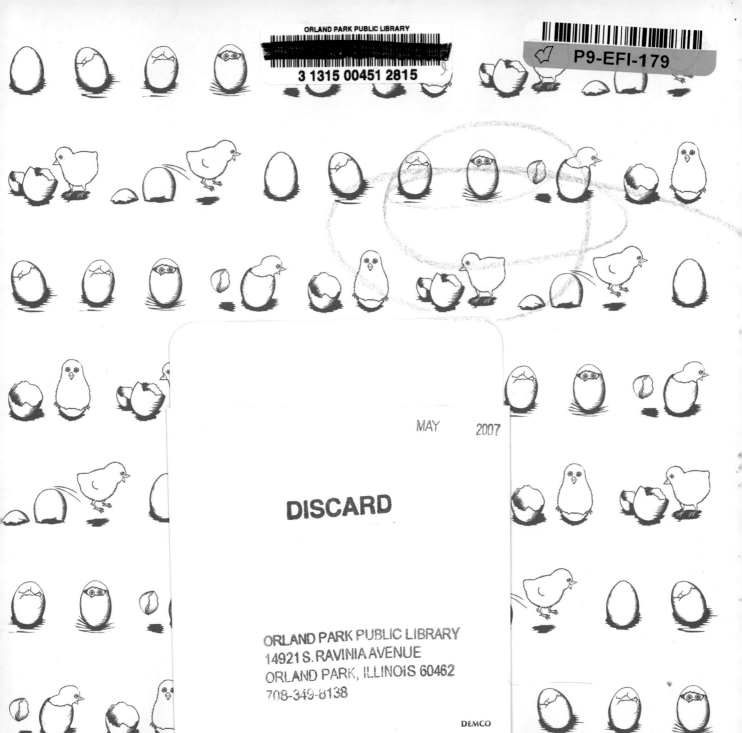

OUT OF THE EGG

To my parents, Keith and Jackie,
who read us all the best stories over and over again

www.houghtonmifflinbooks.com

The text of this book is set in 18-point Legacy Serif.
The illustrations are Japanese woodblock prints, printed by hand.

Library of Congress Cataloging-in-Publication Data
Matthews, Tina (Christina), 1961–
Out of the egg / written and illustrated by Tina Matthews.
p. cm.
Summary: In this version of the familiar tale, Little Red Hen says no when the barnyard
animals whose parents refused to help her plant and tend a seed want to play under the
"great green whispery tree" that she grew, but her chick thinks her answer is mean.
ISBN-13: 978-0-618-73741-3 (hardcover)
ISBN-10: 0-618-73741-3 (hardcover)
[1. Folklore. 2. Animals—Folklore.] I. Title.
PZ8.1.M436Out 2007   398.2—dc22   [E]   2006009812

Manufactured in China
SCP   10   9   8   7   6   5   4   3   2   1

E
MAT

OUT OF THE EGG

TINA ● MATTHEWS

HOUGHTON MIFFLIN COMPANY BOSTON 2007

One day a Red Hen found a green seed.

"Who will help me plant the seed?" she asked.

"Not I," said the Fat Cat.

"Not I," said the Dirty Rat.

"Not I," said the Greedy Pig.

"Then I shall plant it myself,"
said the Red Hen.

And she did.

Soon the seed began to sprout, but the sun was hot and it shone down on the seedling day in and day out.

"Who will help me water the seedling?" asked the Red Hen.

"Not I," said the Fat Cat, said the Dirty Rat, said the Greedy Pig.

"Then I shall water it myself," said the Red Hen.

And she did.

Every day the Red Hen fetched water, but as the tree grew up, so did the weeds around it.

"Who will help me dig out the weeds?" asked the Red Hen.

"Not I," said the Fat Cat, said the Dirty Rat, said the Greedy Pig.

"Then I shall dig them out myself," said the Red Hen.

And she did.

The winter came with the wind and the rain.

"Who will help me shelter the tree?" asked the Red Hen.

"Not I," said the Fat Cat, said the Dirty Rat, said the Greedy Pig.

"Then I shall shelter it myself," said the Red Hen.

And she did.

Through wild days and mild months and
slow-turning years, the tree grew bigger.
And one warm spring day the Red Hen found
a safe place…

...and laid a perfect white egg.

Out of the egg hatched a little red chick.

And in good time a little cat, a little rat, and a little pig came out of the house and walked past the Red Hen on the hill.

"Who will let us in to play under the tree?" said the little cat, said the little rat, said the little pig.

"Not I!" said the Red Hen with a wry smile.

"Mum, that's MEAN!" said the little chick, and everyone else was very quiet.

The Red Hen looked from the little cat and the little rat and the little pig to her own little chick.

"Perhaps it is," she said softly. "Do you think that I should ask them in?"

"No, I shall ask them myself,"
said the little red chick.
   And she did.

So the little cat, the little rat, the little pig,
and the little chick played all day around and
about the great green whispery tree.

And when it was time to go home...

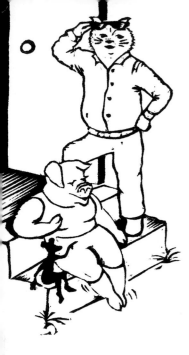

. . . the Red Hen gave them each a green seed.

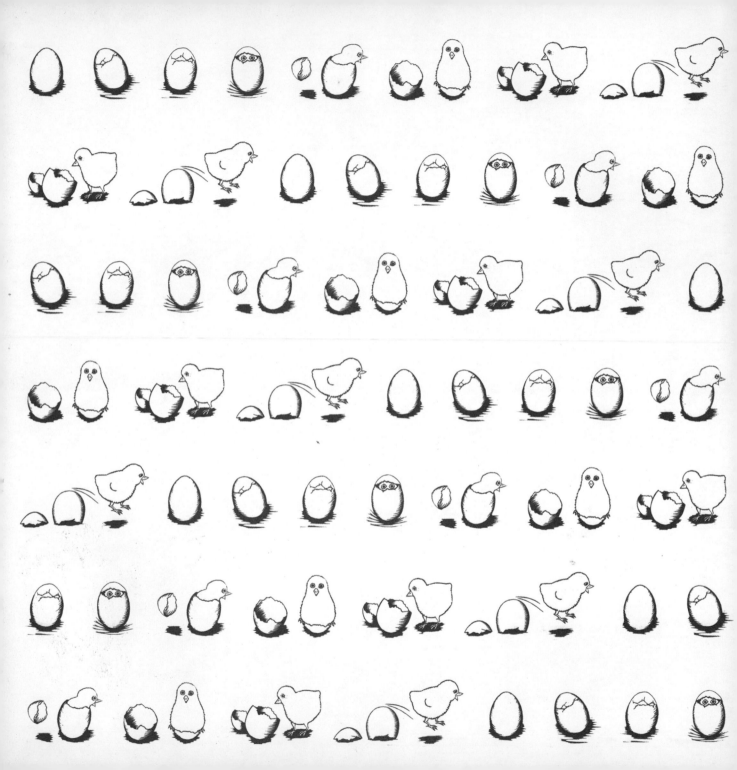